Davide Cali has published over sixty books for children, including *The Queen of the Frogs* (Eerdmans). His work has been published in twenty-five countries, and he has won numerous awards, including the Baobab Prize in 2005 and a BolognaRagazzi Special Award in 2006. Cali was born in Switzerland and now lives in Italy.

Marco Somà was born in Italy. He studied painting at the Academy of Fine Arts in Cuneo and is now a professor of illustration at the same academy. He also illustrates books for children, including *The Queen of the Frogs* (Eerdmans).

First published in the United States in 2017 by Eerdmans Books for Young Readers,
an imprint of Wm. B. Eerdmans Publishing Co.
2140 Oak Industrial Dr. NE, Grand Rapids, Michigan 49505
www.eerdmans.com/youngreaders

Originally published in Italy in 2016 under the title *Il richiamo della palude*
by Kite Edizioni S.r.l.
www.kiteedizioni.it
© 2016 Kite Edizioni
This English translation © 2017 Laura Watkinson

Text by Davide Cali
Illustrations by Marco Somà

23 22 21 20 19 18 17   1 2 3 4 5 6 7 8 9

Manufactured at Tien Wah Press in Malaysia

ISBN 978-0-8028-5486-5

A catalog record of this book is available from the Library of Congress.

Display type set in Sketch Serif
Text type set in Jura

Davide Cali & Marco Somà

The Call
of the
Swamp

Translated by Laura Watkinson

Eerdmans Books for Young Readers

Grand Rapids, Michigan

When his parents found him, they had no children, and they had given up hope that they would ever have any.

The doctors had been clear: *It's impossible*, they'd said. *You can't have children.*

So when the couple found a newborn at the edge of the swamp, it seemed like a gift from heaven, and they paid no attention to the fact that he had gills like a fish.

They didn't know if he had been abandoned or if he had lost his parents, but it didn't matter, because he had found a new mom and dad now.

They called him Boris.

Boris grew up. It didn't matter that his eyes were bigger than everyone else's. He played, ate, and laughed just like all children do.

He learned how to ride a bike and how to climb trees, and then he went to school to learn lots of other useful things.

And some useless things too.

Years went by, and you could say that they were happy years.

Or at least they weren't unhappy.

Then one day, quite unexpectedly, it happened. The wind was blowing, and the air had a salty smell that Boris had forgotten, or maybe had never really known. A scent buried away in the depths of his memory, one he had smelled when he was small. The scent of the swamp.

Boris found himself wondering what his life would have been like if he had stayed in the swamp.

"Why did you take me home, Mom?"

"Because we loved you," she replied.

"But why didn't you leave me where I was?"

"Because you could have died," his dad said.

So many questions whirled around inside his head.

Was he really happy? Was the life he had the one he really wanted? Or was it what other people wanted for him?

Boris could not sleep.

He woke up in the dead of night, feeling like he was suffocating.

And he was thirsty. Always thirsty.

Early one morning, Boris left the house.

He walked and walked.

It was only when his feet felt wet that he knew he had arrived
at the swamp.

He had followed the scent.

Boris realized that he had been living a life that did not belong to him, in a world that was not his own.

His world was the swamp. His scent was the scent of the swamp. He should have been living with other creatures who had gills, like he did.

Boris had never imagined that anyone else like him existed.

But lots of creatures living in the swamp had gills and big eyes just like he did. He found out that they liked the same things. Boris laughed with them like he had never laughed before.

He thought he had found a new family. His real family.

His mom and dad hadn't forgotten him, though. They often went to the swamp and left messages for him hanging from the trees.

The messages never said: *Please come home*.

They simply said: *If you're happy where you are, then we're happy too*.

How much are we really like those who look like us? It's hard to say.

After a while, Boris started to notice differences between himself and the others who lived in the swamp.

They didn't eat the same things as he did, and they talked in a different way. They laughed differently too.

Suddenly he missed the smell of home. It wasn't any scent in particular. It was more like a kind of homesickness, a feeling that seemed to tickle and prickle inside his nose, a feeling that brought back happy memories.

So Boris left his new family.

Maybe, he thought, *it's just me. Maybe I don't belong anywhere. Maybe that's why I don't have a family.*

With that thought, he sank into the swamp and walked along the bottom until he was lost.

Down at the bottom of the swamp, Boris found lots of bottles. They looked empty at first—but no, inside each one was something small and thin. A note.

All of the notes said: *If you're happy where you are, then we're happy too.*

How much like us do those we love have to be?

The question darted around inside Boris's head like a little fish.

His mom and dad had wanted him even though they didn't have gills. It didn't matter that their son didn't look like them.

Maybe our family is simply the ones we love? And the ones who love us back?

Thinking about these questions, Boris left the swamp.

He paused for a moment to breathe in the swampy scent once more.

And then he began to walk toward town.